Mr Bear
BABYSITS

Debi Gliori

ORCHARD BOOKS

*For Leslie Gardiner,
my dear friend,
with lots of love.*

ORCHARD BOOKS
338 Euston Road, London NW1 3BH
Orchard Books Australia
Level 17/207 Kent Street, Sydney, NSW 2000
First published in 1994 by Orchard Books
This edition published in 2009 for Index Books Ltd.
ISBN: 978 1 84616 431 6
Text and illustrations © Debi Gliori
The right of Debi Gliori to be identified as the author and illustrator
of this work has been asserted by her in accordance with the Copyright,
Designs and Patents Act, 1988.
A CIP catalogue record for this book is available from the British Library.
Printed in China
1 3 5 7 9 10 8 6 4 2
Orchard Books is a division of Hachette Children's Books,
an Hachette UK company.
www.hachette.co.uk

"It's no use," said Mrs Bear.
"I can't seem to settle the baby."
"Mmm?" said Mr Bear.

"I can't take her with me to babysit for the
Grizzle-Bears," said Mrs Bear. "She'd keep them
all awake."

"Mmm-hmm," said Mr Bear.

"So you'll have to babysit instead of me," said Mrs Bear.

"Mmm," said Mr Bear. "WHAT?"

So Mr Bear set off for the Grizzle-Bears and knocked on the door. Before he could say, "I've come to babysit," a baby Grizzle-Bear was thrust into his arms.

"We're late, so late, so terribly late," said Mr and Mrs Grizzle-Bear as they bolted out of the door.

"This baby's soggy," said Mr Bear.
"Bathtime!" said a small bear appearing by his side.
Mr Bear didn't know how to bath a baby. His wife
had always taken care of that kind of thing.

"You're not very good at that," said Fred, as Mr Bear climbed into the bath with the baby.

"That's not the right way to do it," said Ted, as Mr Bear dried himself and the baby with the bathmat.

"You're not a proper babysitter," said Fuzz, as the baby started to cry.

Mr Bear didn't know how to stop babies from crying.
He rocked the baby and patted her head.
"You're not very good at that," said Fred.
So Mr Bear tried to sing a lullaby.

"Twinkle, twinkle little slug,
Leaving slime trails on the rug..."

"Those aren't the right words," said Ted.

"You're not a proper babysitter," said Fuzz.
The baby went on crying.
"Perhaps she's hungry?" said Mr Bear.
And he headed towards the kitchen.

"It really is very peaceful,"
sighed Mr Bear as he settled down
into a comfortable chair. "I wonder
what the others are doing?"

BONGA BONGA TWANGGG CRRRASHHH!

The baby woke up and began to cry.

"We were playing hide-and-seek," said Fred.

"...but Fuzz hid in the clock," cried Ted.

"...and it fell over," wailed Fuzz.

"THAT'S IT!" shouted Mr Bear.

"You're quite good at shouting," said Fred.

"UPSTAIRS. BED. NOW!" roared Mr Bear.

"That's the right way to do it," said Ted.

"AND NOT A PEEP OUT OF ANY OF YOU, OR THERE WILL BE TROUBLE!" boomed Mr Bear.

"You *are* a proper babysitter after all," said Fuzz.

And they ran off and dived into bed.

Then… Mr Bear and the baby went back
to the bathroom.
Mr Bear washed and brushed the baby brilliantly.

Next... Mr Bear and the baby went into the kitchen.
Mr Bear cleaned up the mess, made a cup of tea and
warmed some honey for the baby, humming all the while.

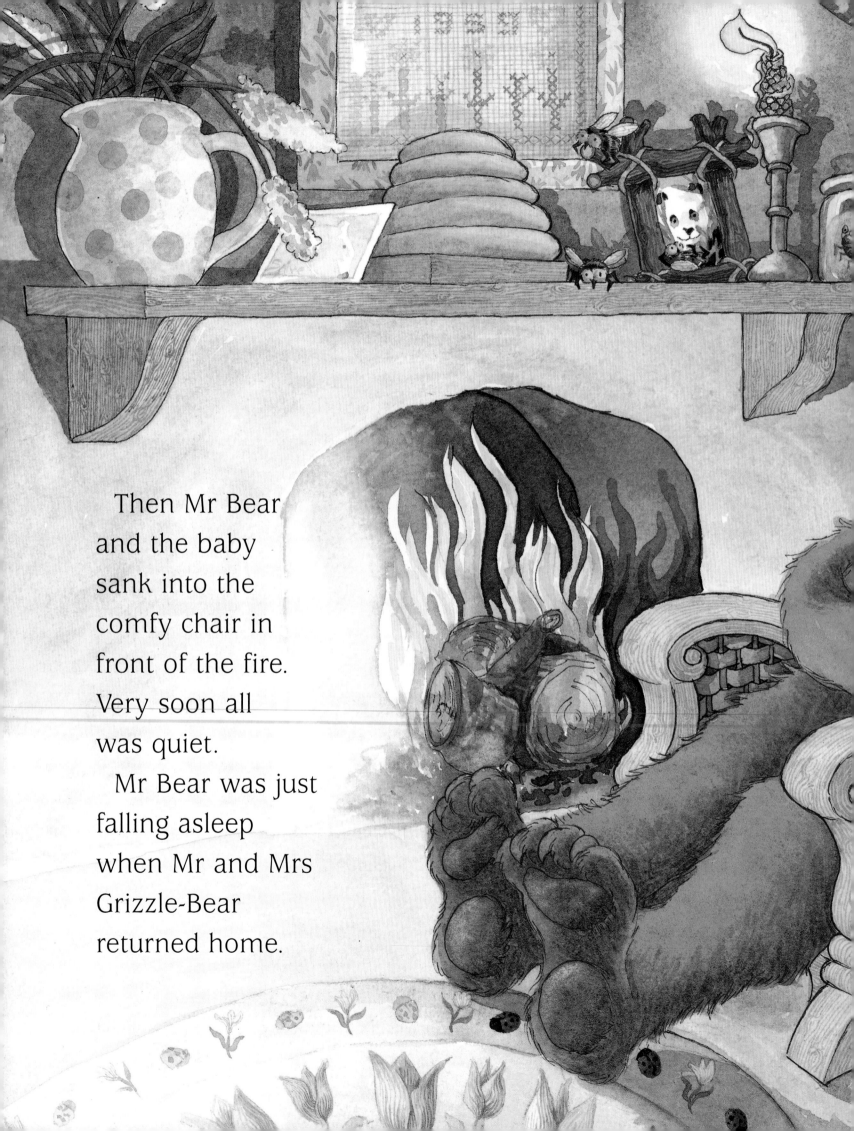

Then Mr Bear
and the baby
sank into the
comfy chair in
front of the fire.
Very soon all
was quiet.

Mr Bear was just
falling asleep
when Mr and Mrs
Grizzle-Bear
returned home.

"Don't know *how* you got that baby to sleep," said Mrs Grizzle Bear. "I always let my husband take care of that kind of thing."

Mr Bear smiled a secret
smile to himself.

Mr Bear walked home by moonlight past burrows
and nests where babies and children were settling
down for the night.

Mr Bear's secret smile grew wider.

When he reached home, Mr Bear
could hear his own baby *still* crying.
He tiptoed inside.

"Can I help?" he said.
"Could you hold her for a
minute, while I make us both a cup
of blueberry tea?" said Mrs Bear.

So Mr Bear held their baby in his lap and sang her a lullaby.

Her cries turned to little hiccupy sobs,
and then to hiccups, and finally, with a small burp,
she closed her eyes.

When Mrs Bear brought in the tea,
she found Mr Bear and their baby fast asleep.